Kitten Wish

ROSIE BANKS

Wishing Star Palace

The Secret Princess Promise

"I promise that I will be kind and brave,

Using my magic to help and save,

Granting wishes and doing my best,

To make people smile and bring happiness."

🐾 CONTENTS 🐾

CHAPTER ONE
Home Run

Charlotte Williams blew her curly brown hair out of her eyes and tightened her grip on the bat. This was it. There were only two minutes left. If she scored a run, her team would win!

She could hear her team-mates calling out and she knew her family would be cheering from the stands. The pitcher threw the ball.

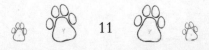

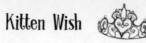

Charlotte swung the bat but missed.

"Strike!" the umpire called.

Charlotte bit her lip. She didn't want to miss again.

The pitcher threw again and the ball came hurtling towards Charlotte.

Thwack!

She hit the ball and sent it flying high up into the air.

She sprinted around the bases.

"Go, Charlotte! Go, Charlotte!" her team-mates shrieked.

From the corner of her eye, Charlotte spotted a player throwing the ball. She ran as fast as she could – and slid into home base just before the catcher caught the ball in her glove.

She'd done it! The umpire blew a blast on the whistle to finish the game. Her team had won by one run!

Charlotte's team-mates raced over. "That was awesome!" gasped Leah, one of Charlotte's new friends.

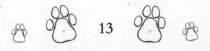

Coach Jacobson high-fived her. "Great work, Charlotte!" he said. "It sure is hard to believe you didn't play softball until this season."

"Didn't you play when you lived in England?" Leah asked curiously.

"Nope," said Charlotte. "In England I played rounders and netball."

"Do you miss playing those games?" Leah asked her.

Charlotte shook her head. "One of the best things about moving to California has been trying lots of new sports!" She grinned. "And the sunshine, of course!"

Coach Jacobson clapped his hands. "Time to get changed, ladies."

The team headed to the locker room. Charlotte's mind was buzzing. Her softball top was dirty, but the game had been so much fun. She couldn't wait to tell Mia about it.

Mia was her best friend. She was back in England, and leaving her had been the hardest thing about moving to California. Luckily, the two friends had discovered they could still see each other in an amazing way – using magic!

Before Charlotte had left for California, their old babysitter, Alice, had given them matching friendship necklaces. Every so often, the necklaces would start to glow. Whenever that happened, the magic began!

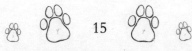

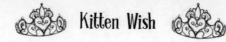

Charlotte and Mia would be whisked away
to a secret place high in the clouds called
Wishing Star Palace. Alice had explained
that they had been selected to train as
Secret Princesses – special girls who could
magically help people by granting wishes.

Charlotte reached the locker room and
took her clothes into a cubicle to get
changed. As she changed her softball top
for a lilac T-shirt she touched her necklace
with its half-heart shaped pendant.

*Oh, I hope Mia and I get to meet up again
soon*, she thought longingly. Just then,
her pendant started to glow. Charlotte
squealed and then clapped a hand over
her mouth, hoping no one had heard.

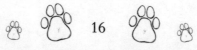

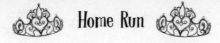
The magic was working again!

Charlotte clutched
the pendant.
"I wish I could
see Mia!" she
whispered.

Light swirled
out of the
necklace and
Charlotte felt herself

being whisked away. She spun
round in a tunnel of light and landed
on soft grass. Opening her eyes, she saw
flowerbeds filled with gorgeous blooms,
a velvet-soft lawn and trees hung with
candyfloss and rainbow-swirled lollipops.

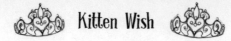

The gorgeous golden turrets of Wishing
Star Palace towered in the distance.

It was so good to be back! Her clothes
had magically transformed into a
beautiful pink princess dress
and strappy silver
sandals. Charlotte
spun around,
her full skirt
twirling around
her legs.

"Charlotte!"
Mia appeared
out from
behind a tall
lollipop tree.

She waved and ran over. She was wearing her golden princess dress with a pretty ribbon. Her diamond tiara glittered in the sun. She giggled. "Did you land in a flowerbed? You've got mud on your nose."

Charlotte grinned. "I'd just finished playing softball when the magic whisked me away."

She rubbed the mud from her nose and straightened her own tiara.

When they had passed the first stage of their Secret Princess training – by granting four people's wishes – their plain tiaras had transformed into sparkling diamond tiaras. Now, they were on the second stage of their training. They needed to grant four more wishes, so that they could earn four rubies. If they did that, they'd get beautiful jewelled ruby slippers that could transport them anywhere by magic!

"We just need to grant two more wishes to get our magic slippers," Charlotte said.

"I hope we can help someone today," said kind-hearted Mia. Charlotte grinned

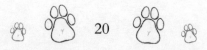

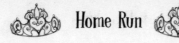

and linked her arm through her best friend's. It was so amazing to see Mia again!

Suddenly they heard the sound of chattering voices. A group of princesses came hurrying across the grass. Alice was leading the way, carrying a rolled-up picnic blanket. She was wearing a red dress and her necklace had a pendant with a musical note on it. When she saw the girls she waved happily. "Charlotte! Mia! You're here just in time!"

"In time for what?" Charlotte asked.

Alice's eyes sparkled. "For the Butterfly Picnic, of course!"

Alice and the other princesses ran over and hugged Charlotte and Mia happily.

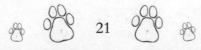

All of the princesses had jobs as well as being Secret Princesses. Back in the real world, Alice was a pop star. Each of the princesses' necklaces showed what their own special talent was – Princess Sylvie had a

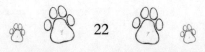

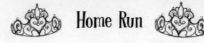

cupcake pendant because she was brilliant at baking, Princess Sophie had a paintbrush because she was an amazing artist, Princess Cara had a thimble because she was a fashion designer, and Princess Evie had a flower because of her gift for gardening.

Charlotte and Mia's talent was for friendship, which was why they had half-heart pendants. They had been told that they were Friendship Princesses – a very rare and powerful type of Secret Princess who always worked as a pair.

"You're going to love the Butterfly Picnic!" said Princess Evie.

"Oooh! What happens?" Mia asked. She loved anything to do with animals.

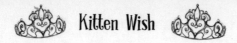

Alice grinned. "You'll have to wait and see. First we have to get to the Wildflower Garden, though." She waved her wand and her blanket spread itself out on the ground. "Sit down, everyone!"

The other princesses quickly sat down on the blanket. Exchanging confused looks, Charlotte and Mia joined them. They had no idea what was going on, but at Wishing Star Palace anything was possible!

CHAPTER TWO
A Very Special Picnic

Princess Alice smiled at the girls and pulled out her wand.

"Picnic blanket, rise and fly
To where butterflies fill the sky!"

She tapped the blanket. It gave a little shake and started to rise up into the air.

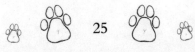

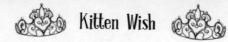
"Oh, wow," breathed Mia, looking over the edge as the blanket started to float across the grounds.

"It's like being on a magic carpet!" said Charlotte, as the blanket bobbed up and down gently. They floated on, over some tennis courts and past a bouncy castle that looked just like a smaller version of Wishing Star Palace. Charlotte wished they could stop and have a go – she loved bouncy castles!

"Look, there's the pond!" Mia said, pointing down.

Far below them colourful flamingoes stood in the water while giant tabby cats snoozed on the grass in the sun. Peacock-like birds

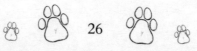

strutted about, opening their beautiful
rainbow-coloured tails.

"That's where Princess Poison's horrible
parrot stole Princess Ella's wand," Mia said.

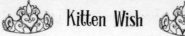

Charlotte glanced over at Princess Ella, who was sitting across the picnic blanket.

She was wearing a light blue dress and had a pawprint pendant on her necklace. She was a vet back in the real world, and she loved animals even more than Mia did.

"Don't worry," Charlotte said, squeezing Mia's hand reassuringly. "We'll get it back from Princess Poison."

Princess Poison was a Secret Princess who had turned bad. She used her magic to ruin people's wishes so she could get more powerful. But since Charlotte and Mia had become trainee Secret Princesses, they had managed to stop her evil plans. The one thing they hadn't been able to do

yet was get Princess Ella's wand back. And
if Princess Poison used the wand to spoil
someone's animal wish, Princess Ella would
be banished from Wishing Star Palace –
for ever!

We won't let that happen, Charlotte
thought determinedly. *Next time we see
Princess Poison, we have to get Ella's wand.*

"We're almost there!" Princess Sophie
called out. "I can see the summerhouse!"

The picnic blanket floated towards a
walled garden. Inside the walls were beds
of beautiful wildflowers and there was a
little wooden summerhouse in the centre.
As they floated over the wall, Charlotte
heard a pretty chiming, tinkling sound.

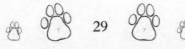

She realised it was
coming from
dozens of wind
chimes
hung all
around the
porch.

The
blanket
floated down
and landed.

"We're here!" said Alice, jumping to her feet. "It's time for our picnic!"

Charlotte's tummy gave a rumble. She was hungry after her softball game but none of the princesses had brought picnic baskets.

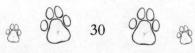

What were they going to eat?

Princess Sylvie waved her wand and called:

> "Picnic feast, now appear.
> Lay out treats over here!"

Charlotte and Mia gasped as two large wooden tables appeared on the summerhouse's porch. They were laden with plates of dainty sandwiches, iced biscuits shaped like butterflies, cupcakes decorated with delicate flowers made out of sugarpaste and crystal glasses of a delicious-looking fruit smoothie.

"Help yourselves, everyone!" said Sylvie.

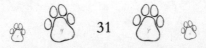

31

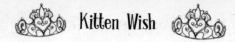

Charlotte and Mia joined the laughing and chattering princesses as they piled their plates high. Then they sat on the picnic blanket in the sun.

"Everything's so yummy," said Charlotte. "This is the best picnic ever!"

As she spoke a warm breeze began to blow and the wind chimes started to tinkle more loudly. The pretty sound swelled through the air.

"The butterflies are coming!" cried Princess Ella. "Look, everyone!" She pointed upwards.

Charlotte peered into the blue sky. For a moment, it looked like thousands of pieces of confetti were floating down towards her, but then she realised it was clouds and clouds of beautiful butterflies! Some were large, others were small. They swooped around the garden in a colourful cloud, fluttering around the princesses' heads and landing on the flowers.

"They're so beautiful!" breathed Mia.

"I knew you'd like them," Princess
Ella said, smiling at her. "They
come here once a year when they are
migrating from north to south. They love to
drink nectar from these wildflowers."

"So they're having a picnic too!" grinned
Charlotte.

A large pale-blue butterfly flitted past
her nose. Mia held out her hand and the
butterfly landed on it. Its silky wings had
dark blue edges and lilac spots at the tip.
"You're gorgeous," she told it, looking at its
tiny eyes and waving antennae.

Three sweet little pink butterflies chased
each other around Charlotte's head.

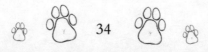

"They're so pretty," she said.

"They may look delicate, but did you know that butterflies are actually really strong?" said Princess Ella. "They can carry fifty times their own body weight with their feet. That's like an adult person being able to carry two cars!"

Charlotte stared at her in amazement. "That's amazing!"

"I know something else about butterflies," added Mia as a small lilac butterfly joined the large pale-blue butterfly. "Some of them can taste with their feet!"

Princess Ella nodded. "You're right. They do that to find out if the leaf they have landed on is a safe place to lay their eggs."

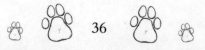

The lilac and blue butterflies flew off
Mia's hand.

"You're not tasty enough for them, Mia,"
Charlotte said with a giggle. Her face lit up.
"Hey, I've just thought of a joke! What do
butterflies learn at school?"

"What?" said Mia.

"*Mothe*matics, of course!" said Charlotte.
Mia and Princess Ella both groaned.

"That's awful, Charlotte," said Mia.

"OK, I'll think of another," Charlotte
said. "Let's see …"

But just then, Princess Ella gasped. "Look,
everyone – your wands!"

The wands had started to glow. "Someone
must need a wish granting!" said Alice.

"We'll have to go back to the palace."

"Why don't Mia and I go?" Charlotte offered. "We can try and grant the wish."

Mia nodded. "We really want to get our next ruby," she said, holding up her pendant. It had two rubies, showing the two wishes they had successfully granted, but there was room for two more.

"I can take the girls to the palace," said Princess Ella.

"It seems a shame for everyone else to abandon the picnic."

"OK, if you're sure," said Alice. "Good luck, girls!"

"And make sure you watch out for Princess Poison," said Princess Cara. "She's bound to try and stop you."

"She's the one who'd better watch out for us!" declared Charlotte.

Mia nodded. "And we're going to try and get Princess Ella's wand back."

Princess Ella gave her a grateful look. "Thank you, girls. But the most important thing is making someone happy and making their wish come true. Let's go and find out who it is!"

Kitten Wish

She held out her hands. Charlotte and
Mia linked hands with her.

"To the Mirror Room!" cried Princess
Ella, tapping her heels together.

She and the girls twirled up into the air
and the magic shoes
whisked them
away.

Charlotte,
Mia and
Princess
Ella landed
inside a
room in
one of the
palace's towers.

Against one wall was an oval mirror in a golden stand. In the glass there was an image of an unhappy-looking girl with curly black hair and brown eyes. She was cuddling a tiny grey kitten with pointed ears and huge green eyes.

A message was scrolling across the glass. Charlotte read it out:

"A wish needs granting, adventures await,
Call Hannah's name, don't hesitate!"

"The girl who needs our help is called Hannah," said Mia. "But why does she look so sad? That kitten she's cuddling is completely adorable!"

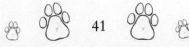

"Maybe she's sad because of something to do with the kitten," said Princess Ella thoughtfully.

"There's only one way to find out," said Charlotte. "Are you ready, Mia?"

Mia nodded and took her hand. "Let's make a wish come true!"

CHAPTER THREE
A Summer Fête

Charlotte and Mia were swept away in a tunnel of light. They arrived in a grassy field, surrounded by people. The girls looked around in amazement. There was a cake stall, a craft stand, an ice cream van, a ring toss and a coconut shy. Kids with painted faces were running around and adults were sitting at tables drinking tea

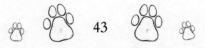

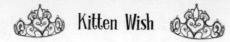
or buying things at the stalls.

"I think we're at a summer fête," said Charlotte.

No one seemed to notice their sudden arrival, but that was part of the Secret Princess magic. Another part of the magic was that their princess dresses and tiaras had transformed into normal summer clothes – just perfect for a sunny day trip!

"Hannah must be here somewhere," said Mia. "Let's try and find her."

They set off around the fête, glancing round at all the stalls.

"Look at all those animals!" said Mia, pointing to an area with a big banner saying WILLOW FARM above it.

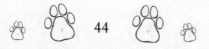

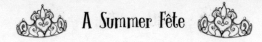

There were pens of lambs and goats, a miniature chestnut Shetland pony and a sheep dog snoozing under the shade of a tree.

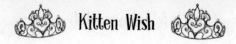

Just then a girl came out of a small tent by the animal pens. She was wearing a bright green polo shirt that said 'Willow Farm' on it.

Mia nudged Charlotte. "That's Hannah!"

Excitement fizzed through Charlotte. This was their chance to discover how they could help her.

Hannah smiled at them as they went over. "Hi there," she said. "I'm Hannah. Feel free to stroke any of the animals – they come from my family's farm. We've brought the friendliest ones out to make a special petting zoo!"

"I'd love to live on a farm," said Mia as she stroked a cute fluffy lamb.

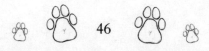

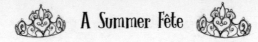

"It's brilliant," agreed Hannah. "Do you like animals, then?"

"I love them!" said Mia.

"Me too, though I don't know as much about them as Mia does," said Charlotte. "I'm Charlotte, by the way, and that's Mia."

Hannah smiled. "If you both like animals, come and look over here!" She beckoned them over to where there was a large pet carrier on a table. The girls peered through the mesh and caught their breath. There were four kittens inside: one stripy ginger one, one fluffy white one, one black and white and one tiny grey tabby.

"Oh my gosh, they're just so cute!" squealed Mia delightedly.

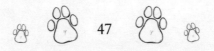

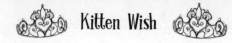

Hannah moved the hay bales to make a
little enclosure, then carefully took them
out. "This is Splodge," she said, handing
Charlotte the black and white kitten.
"He likes chasing things." She wiggled a
stalk of hay near him and the little kitten
pounced on it.

"And this is Titch," she added, giving Mia the stripy ginger kitten. "He's quiet but he loves cuddles. And that's Snowy – she's really friendly and loves playing." She pointed at the white kitten. "And this," she said as she cuddled the little grey one close, "is Daisy." She kissed the kitten's head. "Daisy was really poorly when she was born and I had to bottle-feed her for a while. I still give her extra cuddles."

"You're so lucky to have them!" Mia exclaimed. "They're all so cute!"

"Oh, they're not mine," said Hannah, her face falling. "Mum and Dad say we already have enough animals. I brought them here today to try and find them new homes."

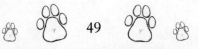

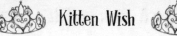
She looked suddenly hopeful. "Would either of you like one?"

"I've already got a cat called Flossie and I don't think she'd like it if I got another one," said Mia regretfully.

"And I'd love one, but my brothers are allergic to cats," said Charlotte. She stroked Splodge. A purr rumbled out of him.

Hannah sighed. "My mum says if we don't find homes for them today then we'll have to take them to the cat sanctuary."

"I'm sure the cat sanctuary would find them all good homes," Mia tried to reassure her.

"I know." Hannah bent down to kiss Daisy's head again. "But I just wish

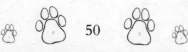

I could meet their owners and make sure they're nice. I want to find really lovely families for them all."

Charlotte and Mia exchanged looks. So that was Hannah's wish! "Well, we can help!" said Charlotte brightly.

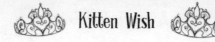

"Yes! What about making leaflets to let people know about them?" said Mia. "We could hand them out."

"That's a good idea," said Hannah. "But I haven't got any paper and pens. And I have to stay here and look after the animals because my parents are taking a break."

"Leave it to us," said Mia.

Hannah gave a huge, beaming smile. "Thank you!" she said.

Charlotte and Mia hurried off. A friendly lady with ginger hair was looking after an arts and crafts stall. When she heard what Mia and Charlotte wanted paper and pens for, she said they could use whatever they needed.

Mia was very good at drawing animals
so she drew pictures of the kittens while
Charlotte did the writing.

"How about: *Four beautiful kittens free
to good homes! One of them is bound to
be just PURR-fect for you, so come to the
Willow Farm animal pens!*" Charlotte said.

"Oh, yes!" said Mia. "That's great!"

They made leaflet after leaflet.

"All done," said Charlotte at last.

They left some of the leaflets with the arts
and crafts lady, who promised to hand them
out to anyone who visited the stall. Then
Charlotte and Mia took a handful of leaflets
each and headed into the crowd. They left a
leaflet with every stall they passed.

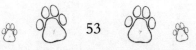

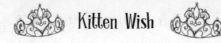

Charlotte looked round. *Who could be the perfect family for a kitten?* she thought. What had Hannah said? Snowy was really friendly, so she'd need a home where people would play with her. She spotted a family with two boys about her brothers' age walking by. "Would you like a kitten?" she said hopefully.

The mum shook her head. "Sorry, love, we already have two dogs."

"If you hear of anyone who does want one, please send them to the Willow Farm enclosure," said Charlotte politely. She saw some mums with buggies passing by and pressed leaflets into their hands. "Kittens looking for good homes!" she said.

She saw that Mia was hesitating, trying to pluck up the courage to approach someone. She was much more shy than Charlotte. "Why don't you ask that lady over there?" Charlotte said, pointing to a kindly-looking older lady with curly grey hair who was working on a stall selling knitted sweaters, scarves and knitted toys. Mia went over to the stall.

"Hi," she said. The lady was wearing a name badge that said JOYCE. "Would you like a leaflet?"

Joyce took the leaflet. "What a super drawing! I love cats, but I haven't had one since my cat, Whiskers, died a little while ago. A kitten might be a bit too much work." She read the words. "But they do sound lovely."

"There's a black and white one," said Charlotte, joining them. "And a white one, a ginger one and a tiny grey one."

Joyce looked tempted. "Whiskers was a ginger cat. And I have been thinking it's time I got another cat. Maybe I *could* give one of these kittens a home."

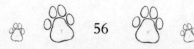

"The ginger one is called Titch, and he's very quiet," Mia said to Joyce. Then she turned and whispered to Charlotte.
"I think they'd be a perfect match."

Charlotte crossed her fingers. "Why don't you come and meet Hannah?" she said.
"She owns the kittens."

"I'll do that. Let me just get my knitting – I've been making a sweater for my little grandson." Joyce carefully packed a little blue sweater, a ball of wool and some knitting needles into a carrier bag and then picked up her handbag too. "All sorted," she said cheerfully. "Lead the way!"

"Hannah! This is Joyce!" called Charlotte, feeling very excited as they took

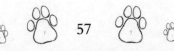

the old lady over to the Willow Farm area.
"She might be able to adopt Titch."

"Really?" Hannah's face lit up. "Do you
want to see him?" She led them to the hay
enclosure. Joyce
looked inside.

"Oh, they're
gorgeous!" she
murmured.
"This is
Titch,"
Hannah
said,
handing
him to
Joyce.

"Well, aren't you just the most precious little bundle of fluff?" Joyce cooed. "I hear you need a home. Would you like to come and live with me?"

Titch rubbed his head against her cheek. Joyce smiled. "I'd love to adopt him," she said to Hannah.

Charlotte exchanged delighted looks with Mia. It seemed like their leaflet idea was working – they'd found a home for one of the kittens and they hadn't even used any magic yet!

"Mum and Dad will be back in a minute and they'll tell you all about the food he's been eating and when his injections are due," said Hannah.

"That would be wonderful," said Joyce.
"I'll nip home – I've got the perfect thing
to carry him home in." Joyce handed Titch
back to Hannah. "I'll be back very soon!"
She hurried off.

"This is brilliant! I'll start writing down
the instructions," Hannah
told Mia and
Charlotte, then
she disappeared
into the tent
with Titch.

Charlotte
and Mia hugged
happily. Titch had
a new home!

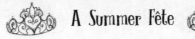
Just then, Charlotte noticed a short, tubby
man beside the goat pen. He had his back
to them and was crumpling up balls of paper
and throwing them at the goats. "What's
that man doing?" she hissed.

Mia frowned. "Oh, no! The goats will eat
the paper and get tummy ache."

Charlotte went over to the man. "Excuse
me," she said politely. "It will make the
goats ill if they eat paper."

"So?" the man said in a rude voice.

Charlotte frowned. She recognised his
voice. Was it …?

The man turned. "Hex!" Charlotte
exclaimed. Hex was Princess Poison's mean
servant.

"Yes, it's me," he said, with a nasty grin.
"And those," he added, pointing into the
pen where the goats were starting to chew
on all the balls of paper, "are all your
precious leaflets!"

CHAPTER FOUR
The Naughty Kitten

Hex sniggered in delight as he saw the shock on their faces.

"You ruined our leaflets?" said Mia.

"Now no one else will find out about the kittens and they won't find homes," Hex said. "You can say goodbye to making a wish come true today!"

He chortled and scurried off into the fête.

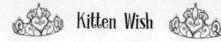

As he passed the table, he knocked Joyce's knitting bag onto the ground. "Whoopsie!" he laughed, not stopping.

"I can't believe it!" Mia said, climbing into the goat pen and picking all the ruined leaflets up so the goats didn't eat them.

Just then Hannah came out of the tent with Titch. "Instructions all done!" She put Titch down on the grass at their feet and then saw their faces. "Are you OK?"

"No, the leaflets we made have been ruined," said Charlotte. She was about to explain when Titch padded over to investigate the bag. Joyce's knitting was poking out of the top. The kitten started patting at it with his front paws.

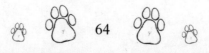

"Don't do that, Titch," said Charlotte quickly, but it was too late. Titch's claws caught in the jumper Joyce was knitting. He pulled back in surprise and the ball of wool rolled out of the bag. He pounced on it and batted it from side to side.

"Titch, you'll ruin
the jumper!"
gasped
Hannah.

They
tried to
grab the
kitten but
he dodged

away from them,
the wool from the wool still caught in his
claws. He bounded away.

"The jumper's unravelling!" gasped
Charlotte. "We've got to catch him!"

They charged after the kitten, but he
thought it was a game and darted this way

and that, leaving a trail of wool tangled
around the pens.

"Got you!" gasped Hannah, cornering
him by the goats' pen. She scooped him up
and untangled his claws. But it was too late
– the jumper was now just a tangled mess of
wool trailing round on the grass.

"Oh, Titch, what a mess!" Hannah
groaned, looking at the spoiled knitting.

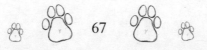

"Oh, it wasn't his fault," Mia said.

"What are we going to do?" Hannah asked the others. "Joyce might not want to adopt him if he's ruined her jumper."

"There's only one thing for it," Mia whispered to Charlotte.

Charlotte nodded, knowing what she was thinking. "It's time for some magic, isn't it?" she whispered back.

Charlotte and Mia pulled their pendants out from inside their T-shirts. The half-hearts were glowing with light.

Hannah stared at the pendants. "Why are your necklaces shining?"

"We'll tell you in a minute," said Charlotte urgently. Joyce could come back

at any second and she didn't want her to see the ruined knitting.

She and Mia joined the pendants together to form a whole heart and Mia whispered, "I wish the wool could turn into a really amazing jumper for Joyce's grandson!"

Light flashed out of the pendants, making them all blink. As they opened their eyes again they saw that the wool on the ground had transformed into a gorgeous blue jumper, perfectly knitted, with an orange dinosaur on the front.

"How did you do that?" Hannah gasped, pointing at the sweater.

Mia picked it up and put it into Joyce's bag. "We used magic," she whispered.

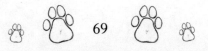

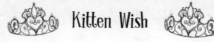

"You mustn't tell anyone, but Charlotte and I are training to become Secret Princesses."

Hannah stared at them, confused.

"It means that we help grant people's wishes," Charlotte explained. "We can't make one big wish, but our necklaces will let us use three small wishes so that we can make sure your kittens find good homes."

"Oh … my … goodness," said Hannah slowly, staring at them as if she was seeing them for the first time. "You can really do magic? Well, of course you can," she went on before they could reply. "I just saw you." She glanced round. "But why didn't anyone else notice?"

"It's part of the magic," explained Mia.

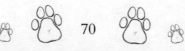

"Joyce won't notice that the jumper is different, either."

"This is amazing!" said Hannah.

Just then Joyce came back carrying a large cat basket. "This was still up in the loft. I've put a blanket inside so it will be lovely and cosy for Titch. Now, are your parents here?"

Hannah pointed to a man and woman dressed in Willow Farm T-shirts and wellies, heading over to the animal pens. "Mum! Dad!" she cried excitedly. "I've found someone who wants to adopt Titch – well, my new friends have."

Hannah's parents came over and she introduced everyone.

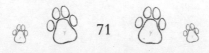

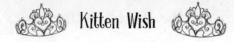

"Hannah's very welcome to come and visit Titch any time," said Joyce.

Joyce opened the door of the basket and Hannah settled Titch inside. She kissed his forehead and shut the door.

Charlotte and Mia grinned at each other.

Titch and Joyce already looked like they belonged together.

"Thanks so much," said Hannah's mum. "I'm pleased Titch has found a good home."

"I promise I'll look after him for you," said Joyce kindly. She picked up her bag of knitting. "Mustn't forget this," she said, setting off with a smile.

"Now we just need to find three more nice people," said Charlotte.

As she spoke, a family came over. There was a mum, a dad and a little girl, who looked about five. She was cuddling a big fluffy toy cat. "Excuse me," said the mum. "We heard that you have some kittens needing homes."

"We do," said Hannah eagerly. "There are three kittens left."

"I really want a kitten," said the little girl longingly. She held up the white toy cat. "Daddy just won this for me. But a real cat would be a million times better."

Her mum smiled. "Ava's been wanting a kitten for ages and I think she's old enough now to help look after it."

"I got my cat when I was about Ava's age," said Mia. She smiled at the little girl.

Hannah had put the kittens safely in the cat carrier, but she let them back out in the hay enclosure so Ava could see them.

Ava caught her breath. "Mummy! Daddy! Look!" She knelt down. Snowy, the white

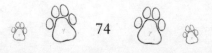

The Naughty Kitten

kitten, trotted over to her and put her paws on her knees. "Can we have this one, Mummy?" Ava begged. "Please!"

Snowy purred.

"She is beautiful," said Ava's mum, looking at her husband. "What do you think, Jim?"

"I think it's a great idea," he said. "Snowy will help teach Ava how to be responsible." He smiled at Hannah. "We often stop at your farm shop to buy eggs and vegetables."

"We can bring you photos of the kitten when we pop in," said Ava's mum.

Hannah beamed. "That would be great, thank you! Do you want to come and meet my mum and dad?"

Ava's parents went off with Hannah.

Ava scooped Snowy into her arms. "Make sure you hold her bottom so she feels safe," said Mia, kneeling down and showing the little girl how to hold the kitten. "And always stroke her fur in the right direction."

"I can't believe I'm going to get a real kitten!" Ava said happily, burying her face in Snowy's soft fur. "I always wanted a white one. They're my favourite."

"Well, well, well, what do we have here?" drawled a cold voice.

Charlotte and Mia looked round. A tall, skinny woman in a green coat was striding towards them. Her dark hair had an ice-blonde streak in it and a green parrot

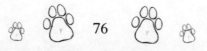

was perched on her
shoulder.

Mia gasped. It was
Princess Poison!

"Go away!"
Charlotte cried.
"We're not going
to let you ruin
Hannah's wish."

"No way," said
Mia, moving to stand
between Princess Poison
and Ava.

"Really?" snapped
Princess Poison, her eyes
glinting nastily.

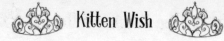

She pulled out Princess Ella's wand and pointed it at Ava. Venom, her parrot, flew off her shoulder and swooped down. For a moment Charlotte thought he was going to grab the kitten, but instead he grabbed Ava's cuddly toy.

"My new toy!" cried Ava as Venom cawed triumphantly and flew away with the stuffed cat in his claws. Ava was still holding Snowy, so she couldn't stop Venom. Instead she burst into tears as the parrot flew away.

"Give that toy back!" Charlotte shouted.

"No!" retorted Princess Poison.

Ava's crying grew louder. A few people nearby looked round.

"Goodness me!" Princess Poison said loudly. "What a vicious kitten! It just bit this little girl and made her cry."

Mia glared at her. "Snowy didn't bite Ava!" She scooped up the little white kitten and put her arm around Ava.

"Well, you would say that," Princess Poison drawled. She snorted, then said loudly, "I can see why the owners want to get rid of them."

All around them, people started to whisper and point. Mia looked like she was about to burst with rage as she held Snowy.

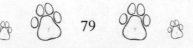

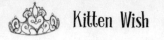

She was usually very calm, but she hated
anyone being mean about animals.

Ava's mum rushed over. "Are you OK,
darling? Did Snowy bite you?"

But Ava was crying too hard to answer.

Charlotte grabbed Mia's arm. "We have
to stop Ava crying, then she can tell her
parents the truth."

Mia took a breath. "Should we use some
Wish Magic?"

Charlotte nodded. But what could they
wish for? Her eyes fell on a ring toss stall
where there was a display of huge stuffed
animals at the back. "Mia!" she gasped.
"I've got an idea!"

CHAPTER FIVE
Hex's Mean Plan

"Don't you dare use your necklaces!"
Princess Poison snarled.

But Charlotte and Mia were already
bringing their glowing half-hearts together.

"I wish that Ava could have one of the
big stuffed toys!" cried Charlotte.

"No!" shrieked Princess Poison in fury.
There was a bright flash and suddenly Ava's

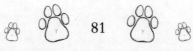

arms were filled with a giant cuddly

white tiger!

Her tears dried

up instantly

and she

hugged it.

"My toy!" she

said, beaming.

Because of

the magic, she didn't notice that the small

stuffed cat had been replaced by something

five times as big.

"Oh!" Ava's mum grinned in relief.

"You were crying about your toy! So Snowy

didn't bite you?"

Ava shook her head. With her tiger under

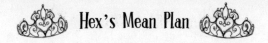

one arm she reached up and gently stroked Snowy, who was still safe in Mia's arms. The little kitten wriggled happily. "I love Snowy," Ava said.

"Would you like to take her home?" her mum asked.

"Yes, please!" Ava said with a grin.

"Gah!" Princess Poison spat. She swung round and stalked off.

Just then, Ava's dad came out of the tent with Hannah, holding a piece of paper and a cardboard box. Ava's dad opened the box and they settled Snowy inside. Hannah stroked her back. "Be good," she told the little kitten. "I want to see lots of lovely photos of you."

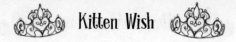

Ava's family said goodbye and set off happily with Snowy.

"We're doing well," said Mia. "That's two of the kittens with new homes."

"Despite Princess Poison trying to stop us," said Charlotte.

"Who's Princess Poison?" asked Hannah curiously.

The girls quickly explained. "She'll do anything to stop your wish from coming true," Charlotte warned.

Hannah shivered. "She sounds horrible."

"She is," said Mia. "But don't worry – we'll find homes for Splodge and Daisy. She won't stop us."

"I'm worried about Daisy," said Hannah.

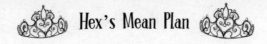

"She's far more timid than the others. I want to find the perfect home for her."

"We will," Charlotte promised. "If only there was a quick way of letting everyone know about the kittens."

As she spoke, there was a loud crackle and a voice came out of a nearby speaker.

"Good afternoon, everyone. I hope you're having a lovely time in the sun. We'll be starting the sack race in ten minutes. Come and join in!"

Charlotte caught her breath. "That's it! Why don't we make an announcement over the loudspeaker system?"

"An announcement?" said Mia, looking a bit nervous.

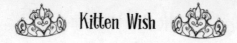

"Don't worry, I'll do it," said Charlotte, grabbing her hand. "Come on!"

"Good luck!" Hannah called after them.

Charlotte and Mia ran through the stalls, dodging round people and buggies. An official-looking man wearing a hat was standing beside a small stage, a microphone in his hands.

"Excuse me," Charlotte said politely.

The man smiled. "Yes! What can I do for you, young lady?"

"We were hoping you could help a friend of ours from Willow Farm." Charlotte explained about Hannah and the kittens. "Could we make an announcement about the two kittens that are left?"

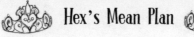

"Of course you can," the man said. He handed the microphone to Charlotte.

Charlotte pressed the button. "Hello, everyone!" she said. She heard her voice booming out around the fête and grinned. This was fun! "There are two adorable kittens looking for new homes at the Willow Farm—" There was a flash of green light and then the microphone screeched and hissed, drowning out her words.

Charlotte tried again. "They're at the Willow—"

SCREECH!

The microphone made an ear-splitting noise. All around the fête people winced and covered their ears.

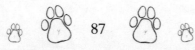

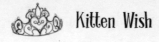

"Charlotte!" Mia pointed. Princess Poison was standing nearby with Princess Ella's wand pointing straight at the microphone. There was a cruel smirk on her face. She must have cast a spell to stop the microphone working.

"I'm very sorry," the man with the hat said, inspecting the microphone as Charlotte handed it back. "I don't know why it made that awful noise. I'll have to get it swapped for another."

"I'm sure it'll be fine in a few minutes," said Charlotte, glaring at Princess Poison, who smiled smugly back at her.

"Come on, we can try something else," Mia said.

The girls headed back over to the Willow Farm area.

"Do you think people heard enough of the message?" Mia asked anxiously.

"Let's hope so," said Charlotte.

Hannah was putting hay in the goat pen.

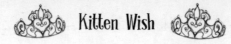

Charlotte and Mia set to work, helping her. They had just finished when a young couple approached.

"Hi, is this where the kittens are?" the man asked. "We heard an announcement but then the sound cut out."

"You've come to the right place," said Charlotte eagerly.

"We'd love to adopt a kitten," said the woman. "We've just moved to an old farmhouse and we need a cat to help keep the mice away."

"I bet Splodge would be perfect," said Mia. "He loves pouncing on things." She called Hannah over. Hannah undid the carrier and took out the black and white kitten.

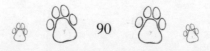

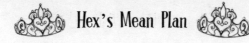

"Oh, he's lovely!" said the lady, taking him from Hannah.

"He's just what we were looking for," agreed the man. "He looks like he'd scare the mice off."

"And he obviously likes cuddles too," said the lady, laughing as Splodge nuzzled into her arm, then lifted a paw to bat at her hair.

The girls giggled at the happy kitten.

The lady turned to Hannah. "If you're happy for us to have him, we'd love to take him home."

Hannah gave a big smile. "That would be great. Come and meet my parents."

Mia and Charlotte grinned as the couple followed Hannah into the tent.

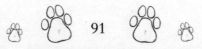

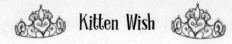

"Just Daisy to go now," said Mia. "But we'd better be quick – everyone's starting to pack up their stalls." She went over to the carrier. "Poor Daisy, you must be feeling lonely in there." She gasped. "Oh, no! Charlotte, come here! Daisy's gone!"

Charlotte ran over. The cat carrier was empty, and so was the hay enclosure. "She can't have just vanished!" Charlotte said.

They heard sniggering and Hex popped out from behind the goat pen.

"Have you done something with Daisy?" Charlotte demanded.

Hex rubbed his hands together. "I let her out and now she's run away!" He giggled. "Now you'll never grant that girl's wish!"

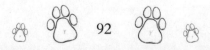

Hex scurried away, laughing.

"What are we going to do?" exclaimed Mia. "Poor Daisy must be so scared!"

"We've got to find her." said Charlotte, her heart pounding as she thought of the timid little kitten being out on her own. "And fast!"

"Let's use our last wish to find where Daisy is," Charlotte said to Mia. But just as they were about to put their pendants together, they heard a faint mewing.

"That's Daisy!" said Mia

"It sounds like she's somewhere above us," said Charlotte, puzzled. She looked around. "Over there!" she gasped, spotting a flash of grey high up in a nearby oak tree.

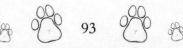

They hurried over to the tree. Daisy was clinging to a branch, digging her claws in and looking terrified.

"She's stuck!" cried Mia in dismay.

"What's going on?" Hannah came running over. "What are you—" She broke off with a gasp. "Oh, no! What's Daisy doing up there?" She grabbed at a branch and started to pull herself up the tree trunk. "It's OK, Daisy," she called, her voice sounding shaky. "I'm coming!"

"Maybe we should get a ladder," said Mia.

"She's scared," Hannah said. "I have to get her now!" She pulled herself up on to the first branch and then reached up for the branch above.

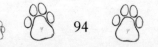

"Hannah, whatever are you doing?" her mum cried, hurrying over.

"Rescuing Daisy, Mum!" panted Hannah. "She can't get down!"

"Oh, poor thing," said Hannah's mum as Daisy gave a scared little mew.

"Be careful, Hannah!" her dad said anxiously.

"I just need to go up one more branch," said Hannah.

"Maybe we should use magic," Mia said nervously as Hannah climbed.

Charlotte bit her lip. "Let's wait a minute – I think Hannah can do it!"

The girls watched as Hannah climbed.

"You're doing really well!" Mia shouted up to her.

Hannah gave them a grateful look. Then, taking a deep breath, she pulled herself up to the next branch, her legs kicking as she scrambled to climb on to it. It wasn't as thick as the lower branches and it wobbled as she stood on it.

"Hannah, be careful!" her dad called.

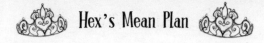

But Hannah's eyes were fixed on Daisy,
clinging to the branch above her.
The kitten stared down with wide green
eyes. "It's all right, Daisy. I'm here,"
Hannah soothed. She balanced carefully on
the branch and
reached up.
Her fingers
closed
around
Daisy's fluffy
body and she
pulled
the kitten
gently into
her arms.

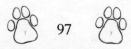

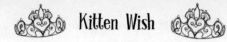

Mia and Charlotte cheered.

"Her heart's beating really fast," called Hannah, stroking the tiny kitten.

There was a loud creak from the branch. "Whoa!" Hannah gasped, grabbing it with one hand as it started to bend.

"Hannah!" her mum cried in alarm.

CRACK!

"The branch is breaking!" Hannah yelled. "Help!"

 98

CHAPTER SIX
A Home for Daisy

"Mia!" Charlotte called out desperately.
The two girls pulled their pendants out and
brought them together as quickly as they
could. Charlotte started to make a wish.
"I wish for a ... a ..." What should she wish
for? Suddenly she knew! "A bouncy castle
under the tree!"

There was a flash of light and a bright

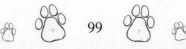

pink and lilac bouncy castle, just like the
one in the Wishing Star Palace grounds,
suddenly appeared!

With another cracking sound the branch
broke and Hannah fell, clutching Daisy
tightly to her chest. She landed safely
on her back on the bouncy castle and the
fear on her face changed to delight.

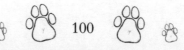

She bounced on to her feet. "Oh, wow!" she cried, looking at Hannah and Mia who grinned back at her.

"Miaow!" said Daisy, purring happily in Hannah's arms.

"Oh, Hannah, thank goodness that bouncy castle was there," said her mum, reaching out her hand to help her.

Hannah clambered off. "I'm OK and so is Daisy."

Her mum and dad pulled her into a hug. "Next time, call an adult," her mum said. She sounded cross, but she kissed the top of Hannah's head.

"It was a very brave thing to do," Hannah's dad added.

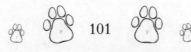

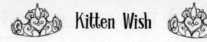

"But please don't do it again!" her mum begged, squeezing her tight.

"I'm sorry, Mum." Hannah stroked Daisy's fluffy grey head. "I just had to rescue Daisy. I couldn't leave her up the tree, she was scared."

"You really love her, don't you?" Hannah's mum said.

Hannah nodded. Tears filled her eyes. "Please can we keep her until I find her a good home, Mum? I want her to have a very special home where she'll be really loved."

"I think we can find a home like that," her dad said. He glanced at Hannah's mum, who nodded. "How about with us?"

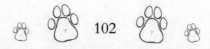

"You mean …" Hannah gave a gasp.
"I can keep her?"

Her mum nodded. "It's obvious how much
you love her and how much she trusts you.
I'm sure we can fit one more animal in."

"Oh, thank you!" Hannah cried. She bent
to kiss Daisy's soft head. "You hear that,
Daisy? You're staying with me, for ever!"

Daisy purred in delight.

Hannah turned to Mia and Charlotte, her
eyes sparkling. "My wish has really come
true and it's all thanks to you!"

They grinned at her.

There was a bright flash and suddenly
hundreds of gorgeous, brightly coloured
blue and yellow butterflies filled the sky.

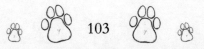

Everyone gasped and pointed as the butterflies swooped and fluttered around their heads in a glowing cloud.

"I'm going to put Daisy in the carrier to take her home," Hannah said, running off.

Her dad smiled. "And we've got lots of other animals to put away, remember!"

Charlotte hugged Mia. "We did it! We granted Hannah's wish!"

"Oh, you two think you're so clever, don't you?" They swung round. Princess Poison was standing behind them with Venom flying overhead and Hex at her side. She glared furiously at Hex. "I thought you told me you'd fixed everything! You said they

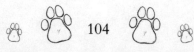

weren't going to able to grant the wish!"

Hex grovelled.

"I'm sorry, Mistress.
I thought—"

"Nincompoop!
Imbecile!" shouted
Princess Poison,
hitting him
on the
head with
Princess
Ella's wand.

"Ouch!"
cried Hex.

"Poopy-ninc!"
squawked the parrot.

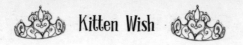

Princess Poison turned to face the girls.
"And you can wipe the smiles off your
faces." She held up the wand. "You may
have granted a wish, but I've still got that
silly princess's wand. As soon as I ruin a
wish, she'll be banished for ever!"

One of the goats trotted over. Hannah's
dad had been so distracted by the cloud of
butterflies that he hadn't noticed it escaping
from the pen.

"Maaa!" The goat grabbed hold of the
back of Princess Poison's green coat and
tried to eat it!

"Get off, you horrible beast!" Princess
Poison cried, flapping at it with her hands.
"Hex! Help me!"

Hex tried
to tug the
coat out of
the goat's
mouth,
but the
goat tugged
stubbornly
back.

RIP!

The coat tore.

The goat munched on a mouthful of green fabric while Princess Poison and Hex both staggered backwards.

Princess Poison shrieked, her arms flailing. Princess Ella's wand flew up into the air.

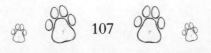

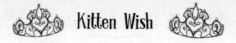

Charlotte saw her chance and sprinted towards it. She leapt up to grab it, but before her fingers could grasp it ...

SQUAWK!

Venom swooped down and snatched the wand from the air. He flew back to Princess Poison and dropped it in her hand.

Charlotte groaned.

"Silly Secret Princesses!" Venom squawked. "Perfect Princess Poison!"

Princess Poison's eyes glinted triumphantly. "As you can see, all my animals are very well trained! Soon your pet-loving princess friend will just be plain old Ella, as soon as I use her wand to spoil someone's wish!"

 108

"We won't let you!" Charlotte started to run towards Princess Poison, intent on grabbing the wand. But Princess Poison waved it and the next instant she, Hex and Venom had disappeared in a flash of green light.

Charlotte stopped in dismay. "Oh no."

Mia caught up and put her hand on Charlotte's shoulder. "Don't worry. We will get it back," she said. "At least we made Hannah's wish come true today."

Hannah came running back to them. "Did you see all those butterflies? Today really has been the best day ever!"

"There's just one thing that will make it even better," said Charlotte.

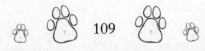

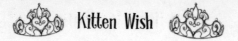

"What?" asked Mia, puzzled.

"A bounce on the bouncy castle!" cried Charlotte, grabbing their hands. Laughing and shrieking, the three of them ran to the bouncy castle and jumped on it. They bounced for ages until they all collapsed, panting, on to the wobbling floor.

"That was so much fun!" Hannah said with a giggle.

Just then the loudspeaker crackled. "Would Mia and Charlotte please come to the cake stall?"

Charlotte and Mia exchanged surprised looks. "Why do we need to go to the cake stall?" wondered Mia.

"We'd better find out," said Charlotte.

"Thank you so much for helping me today," said Hannah.

"It's been lots of fun," said Mia. "And you get to keep Daisy for ever."

"And the other three kittens all have lovely homes, too," said Hannah happily. She lowered her voice. "I'll always believe in magic from now on."

They hugged Hannah goodbye and then Charlotte and Mia hurried to the cake stall.

A familiar figure was standing beside it. "Princess Sylvie!" Charlotte cried.

The red-haired princess was wearing a green top and a spotty skirt. She waved when she saw the girls and offered them each a butterfly cupcake.

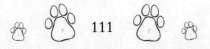

"Thank you!"
said Mia,
grinning
at her.

"They're
not magic,"
whispered

Princess Sylvie, guiding them away from
the other people. "But you must be hungry
after your adventure!"

"They're delicious!" said Mia, biting into
the sweet icing.

"You've done so well granting Hannah's
wish," said Princess Sylvie. "And now it's
time for your reward." She pulled out her
wand and touched it to the girls' pendants.

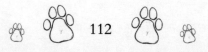

There was a flash of red light and suddenly each pendant had a new, sparkling ruby.

"Just one more to get and then we'll pass the second stage of training," said Charlotte touching the sparkling stone.

"You'll get your final ruby," said Princess Sylvie. "I know you will. But now it's time to say goodbye." She hugged them both. "See you soon."

Mia grinned at Charlotte. "I hope you have fun playing softball."

"I'd almost forgotten about that," said Charlotte.

She and Charlotte hugged and then Princess Sylvie waved her wand. A cloud of sparkles swirled all around them.

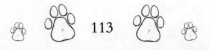

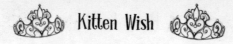

They reminded Charlotte of the cloud of butterflies that had flown down when Hannah's wish had been granted. "Goodbye!" she called as she felt herself being whisked away.

Charlotte spun round and round and then blinked as the sparkles cleared. She was back in the locker room. "Wow," she breathed, hardly able to believe everything that had just happened.

She quickly got changed and hurried outside, where her family was waiting.

"Well done!" her mum said, hugging her.

"You got the winning run!" said her little brother, Liam.

"It was awesome!" said his twin, Harvey.

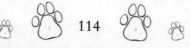

"What an exciting afternoon," her dad said as they started to walk to the car.

A butterfly fluttered past Charlotte's nose and she wondered what her family would say if they knew how exciting her afternoon had REALLY been. "Oh yes," she said, with a grin. "It definitely has been VERY exciting!"

The End

Join Charlotte and Mia in their
next Secret Princesses adventure

Read on for a sneak peek!

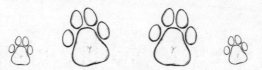

Bunny Surprise

"Can we go and feed the ducks, Mummy?"
Elsie Thompson tugged at her mum's hand
as they walked through the park.

"OK. Let me just grab a coffee from the
café first," her mum said.

"Mum!" Elsie whined.

"I'll take Elsie to the pond, Mum," Mia
offered helpfully.

"Thanks, sweetheart," said Mrs
Thompson, handing Mia a bag of birdseed.

Elsie skipped along beside Mia, her blonde
pigtails bouncing as they set off towards

the pond. Ducks and fluffy yellow ducklings were paddling around on the surface. "I love ducklings, they're so cute!" she said.

"I like the swans," said Mia, pointing to two elegant white swans who were floating across the water.

"What are those fluffy grey ones?" said Elsie, pointing at the birds paddling along behind the swans.

"They're cygnets – baby swans!" said Mia.

Elsie gave Mia a suspicious look. "They don't look like swans. Are you sure?"

"Positive," said Mia with a laugh. "When they get older they'll get white feathers and their necks will grow long."

"You know *everything* about animals!"

Elsie declared.

Mia grinned. She still had lots to learn
if she was going to be a vet when she was
older, but she loved animals.

She and Elsie threw some birdseed into
the water and the ducks squabbled over it.
The girls' mum joined them, a coffee in
her hand.

"Hey, Mum. What time does a duck wake
up?" Mia asked.

"I don't know," said her mum. "When?"

"At the *quack* of dawn!" Mia told her.

Elsie giggled and Mrs Thompson raised
her eyebrows. "Hmm. I bet I can guess who
told you *that* joke. Was it Charlotte?"

Mia nodded. She and Charlotte had

been best friends their whole lives.
When Charlotte had told her that her
family was moving to America, Mia had
been heartbroken. But just before Charlotte
had left, their old babysitter, Alice, had
given them matching necklaces. Each
necklace was made of gold and had a
half-heart pendant on it. The necklaces
weren't just pretty – they were magic! They
could whisk the girls away to an amazing
place called Wishing Star Palace.

But that wasn't the only surprise. When
they'd first visited the palace, Alice had
explained that Mia and Charlotte had
been chosen to train to become Secret
Princesses – special people who could grant

wishes. If Mia and Charlotte completed all the different stages of training they would become Secret Princesses, just like Alice!

Elsie spotted an ice cream van arriving on the far side of the pond. "Can we have an ice cream, Mummy?"

"OK," her mum said. "Do you want one too, Mia?"

"I'll catch up with you in a minute," she said. "I'll feed the ducks the rest of the seed."

"OK." Her mum and Elise set off. After checking that no one was watching, Mia pulled her pendant out from inside her T-shirt. "Oh, wow," she breathed. The half-heart was glowing with light. She was about to have another magical adventure!

"I wish I could see Charlotte!" she
whispered.

Light streamed out of the pendant and
surrounded her, then swept her away. Mia's
heart sang in excitement. Her mum and
Elsie wouldn't even know she was gone – no
time would pass while she was away – the
magic always made sure of that.

Round and round she twirled until she
landed on a pebbly beach. The sky was
the colour of gorgeous forget-me-nots and
little waves lapped against the pebbles of
the curving bay. Best of all, her jeans and
T-shirt had changed into her beautiful
golden princess dress.

"Mia!" Hearing her name, Mia swung

round. Charlotte was running across the
pebbles towards her. She was wearing
a floaty pale pink dress and a diamond tiara
glittered in her curly brown hair.

Read Bunny Surprise
to find out what
happens next!

Princess Ella's Kitten Care Tips

Kittens are the cutest! But owning one is a big responsibility. Are you ready to care for a kitten? Here, Princess Ella explains what a little kitten needs from you.

• Make sure your kitten always has plenty of clean water to drink.

• Ask your vet what to feed your pet. Kittens have small tummies so need to eat little and often. A balanced diet will keep them healthy as they grow.

• Take your kitten to the vet for regular check-ups. Kittens need injections to stop them from getting ill. They also need protection against fleas and worms, which can give them itchy skin and an upset tummy.

• Long-haired cats and kittens need to be brushed gently every day to stop their fur from getting matted. Cats clean themselves with their tongues so you don't usually need to give them baths.

Equipment List:

- Carrier
- Bed
- Food and water bowls
- Collar
- Brush
- Litter tray, scoop and cat litter
- Toys
- Scratching post

Dos and Don'ts

DO get your kitten micro-chipped in case it gets lost.

DON'T let your kitten outdoors until it has had all her injections.

DO remove any houseplants that could be poisonous to your kitten.

DON'T feed your kitten milk as it can upset its tummy.

♥ FREE NECKLACE ♥

In every book of Secret Princesses series two:
The Ruby Collection, there is a special Wish Token.
Collect all four tokens to get an exclusive Best Friends
necklace for you and your best friend!

Simply fill in the form below, send it in with your four tokens
and we'll send you your special necklaces.*

Send to: Secret Princesses Wish Token Offer, Hachette Children's Books
Marketing Department, Carmelite House, 50 Victoria Embankment,
London, EC4Y 0DZ

Closing Date: 31st June 2017

secretprincessesbooks.co.uk

------------------------------✂------------------------------

Please complete using capital letters (UK and Republic of Ireland residents only)

FIRST NAME:

SURNAME:

DATE OF BIRTH: DD | MM | YYYY

ADDRESS LINE 1:

ADDRESS LINE 2:

ADDRESS LINE 3:

POSTCODE:

PARENT OR GUARDIAN'S EMAIL ADDRESS:

I'd like to receive regular Secret Princesses email newsletters and information about other great Hachette Children's Group offers (I can unsubscribe at any time).

Terms and Conditions apply. For full terms and conditions please go to
secretprincessesbooks.co.uk/terms

1 Secret Princesses Wish Token

2000 necklaces available while stocks ▶
Terms and conditions apply.

♥ WIN A PRINCESS GOODY BAG ♥

Secret PRINCESSES

What would you wish for?

Design your own dress and win a Secret Princesses goody bag for you and your best friend!

Charlotte and Mia get to wear beautiful dresses at Wishing Star Palace, but now they want you to design one for them.

To enter all you have to do is follow these steps:

Go to **www.secretprincessesbooks.co.uk**

♥ Click the competition module
♥ Download and print the activity sheet
♥ Design a beautiful dress for Charlotte or Mia
♥ Send your entry to:

Secret Princesses: Ruby Collection Competition
Hachette Children's Group
Carmelite House
50 Victoria Embankment
London
EC4Y 0DZ

Closing date: 31st March 2017
For full terms and conditions,
visit www.hachettechildrens.co.uk/terms

Good luck!

Secret
PRINCESSES

What would you wish for?

Are you a Secret Princess?

Join the Secret Princesses Club at:

secretprincessesbooks.co.uk

Explore the magic of the
Secret Princesses and discover:

♥ Special competitions! ♥
♥ Exclusive content! ♥
♥ All the latest princess news! ♥

Ruby720

Enter the special code above on the website to receive

50 Princess Points